Almost Forever

Almost
Forever

Maria Testa

CANDLEWICK PRESS
CAMBRIDGE, MASSACHUSETTS

Copyright © 2003 by Maria Testa

First paperback edition 2007

The Library of Congress has cataloged
the hardcover edition as follows:

Testa, Maria.
Almost forever / Maria Testa. —1st ed.
p.   cm.
Summary: A young girl describes what she, her brother, and their mother do during the year that her doctor father is serving in the Army in Vietnam.
ISBN 978-0-7636-1996-1 (hardcover)
1. Vietnamese Conflict, 1961–1975—United States—Juvenile fiction. [1.Vietnamese Conflict, 1961–1975—United States—Fiction. 2. Fathers—Fiction. 3. Mother and child—Fiction. 4. Brothers and sisters—Fiction.]   I. Title.
PZ7.T2877 Al 2003
[Fic]—dc21   2002034757

ISBN 978-0-7636-3366-0 (paperback)

2 4 6 8 10 9 7 5 3 1

Printed in the United States of America

This book was typeset in Cheltenham.

Candlewick Press
2067 Massachusetts Avenue
Cambridge, Massachusetts 02140

visit us at www.candlewick.com

For Antonio and Carlo, forever

*Contents

Almost Forever

Christmas 1967

We were all together
decorating
the Christmas tree
the day the orders came
for Daddy,
Special Delivery.

Daddy opened
the envelope
slowly,
unfolded the letter,
and said only one word:
  Vietnam.

Mama sat down
right there
on the floor,

right there
in front of the tree.

    I leave in February,
Daddy said.

It was 1967.
And we never finished
decorating
the Christmas tree.

Doctors Don't Fight

Daddy needed
to explain
to my brother
and me
what doctors do
when they go
to war:

> *Doctors don't fight.*
> *We take care of*
> *the people*
> *who get hurt*
> *in the fighting.*

"Doctors get hurt, too,"
Mama
needed
to say.

"Bullets and bombs
do not care
that you went
to medical school."

Valley View

After Christmas
the four of us moved
three blocks away
from our apartment
near Daddy's hospital
to a government-owned
apartment
in a four-family house
surrounded by other
four-family houses,
all the same.

All the houses
together
were called Valley View,
but there wasn't any valley
and there wasn't any view.

There were
a lot of signs
everywhere—
in the parking lot,
on the buildings,
in the hallways—
signs, everywhere,
printed in
big block letters
stating rules
and regulations
all beginning
with the words
DO NOT.

My brother
read every sign
out loud,

showing off,
but Mama
did not seem
impressed.
"At least the Army
will pay the rent,"
was all she said.

Packing

"I can't help you,"
Mama said
to Daddy
as she folded clothes
and rolled socks.
"I have no idea
how to help
someone pack
his bags
to go to war."

Mama placed
two boxes
of airmail stationery
on top
of a pile
of clothes.

Daddy packed
carefully,

following the list
the Army
had given to him.

Last of all,
in the corner
of a big green duffel bag,
he tucked away
three small framed pictures
of Mama,
my brother,
and me.

I don't want
to forget
what you look like,
Daddy said.
He smiled at me
and I laughed
out loud,
the only one
who thought
Daddy's joke
was funny.

Green Day

And then,
on a snowy day
in February,
all the grandparents
and aunts and uncles
and cousins
came to Valley View
to say goodbye.

Daddy wore
a new green uniform
a new green hat,
and new green boots,
and everyone helped
carry big green duffel bags
out to our car.

All the relatives
surrounded Daddy
for one last hug, one last kiss,
and I saw

my brother
kick
the pile
of green bags
stacked by the curb,
lopsided
in the snow.
"What's not
your favorite color?"
he asked.
"Green,"
I said.

One Year (Not Such a Long Time)

The four of us
gathered
with other families,
we all gathered
in a building
on the Army base,
all in a special room
set aside
for saying goodbye.

*One year
is not
such a long time,*
Daddy said,
kneeling on one knee
in front of me,
squeezing
my shoulders.

*In one year, Baby,
you'll be in*

second grade,
not first,
and you'll be
seven years old,
not six,
and then
I'll be home.
One year
is not
such a long time.

I did not
tell Daddy
that he was wrong—
that second grade
was half a hallway
and a whole world
away from first,
that seven
was everything
six was not,
and that one year
was forever.

Just Like Always

The apartment looked
exactly
the same
as when we
had left it.
Nothing much
changes
in one afternoon.

"Let's have
pancakes
for supper
and go to bed early."
Mama sounded
excited,
almost singing,
like she'd just had
the best idea
in the world.
My brother and I
jumped

into action,
measuring flour,
cracking eggs,
pulling on pajamas.
We had
things to do
after all—
tomorrows to plan
and places to be,
school in the morning
just like always.
Nothing much
changes
in one afternoon.

School Day

No one
looked at me
any differently
at school
the next morning.
No one
asked me
any questions
or said anything
special
at all.

The teachers were the same,
the kids were the same,
and the cafeteria ladies
smiled
the same way they always did
as they scooped up
the macaroni and cheese.

I must have seemed
the same
as always, too,
because
no one
looked at me
any differently
for the whole day,
except once,
during afternoon recess
when I was IT
and I turned around
fast
and stood
face-to-face
with my brother.

I never cared much
about the mail
before,
never cared much
about the envelopes and packages
that were never meant
for me.

But Daddy wrote to us
every day
from Vietnam
and that changed
everything.

My brother and I
raced
every afternoon
to our mailbox,
raced to be
the first
to find

the letter
that was always meant
for us.

Sometimes,
a day or two would pass
with no letter from Daddy,
but then the next day
would come,
and there would be two
or maybe three.

Most of the time
Mama read the letters
to my brother
and me.
Sometimes
she would read
the whole letter
from beginning
to end.
Sometimes
she would stop suddenly
and leave out parts.

Daddy wrote
about lots of different things
like volleyball games
and all the doctors
living in tents
and about how there was not
one nurse
in all of Vietnam
as beautiful
as Mama.

Daddy wrote
about lots of different things
all the time,
but the endings
of his letters were
always,
always
the same:
> *Love you,*
> *miss you,*
> *need you . . .*

Lollipops

Every day after school,
the three of us—
     Mama, my brother,
     and me—
would walk two blocks left
and three blocks right
to the post office.

Every day,
we would join the line
in front of the second window;
it did not matter
if the lines
in front of other windows
were shorter.

Mama liked
the old man
who worked at
the second window.

He always gave us
lollipops
with looped safety sticks,
he'd even give one
to Mama.
"I like these,"
she used to say,
smiling.

Then the old man
would take Mama's letter
to Daddy
into his hands,
saying,
"I'll take
special care
of this."

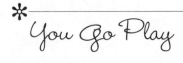

You Go Play

Mama liked
to take us
to the playground
sometimes.
"It's important
for kids
to be kids,"
she'd say.

So we would walk
a short way past
the post office,
and then the three of us
would run,
fast and laughing,
for the last
block and a half
when the playground
came into view.

Mama would inspect
the sandbox
for broken glass
and cigarette butts
and check to see
if the swings
were securely fastened,
or if there were
enough rungs
on the ladder
to climb to the top
of the tallest slide.

And then,
on the best days,
she'd smile and say,
"You go play,"
and my brother
would take off
running
and I'd chase after him

while Mama followed
close behind,
whistling and shouting
about how
she never saw
a little boy
run so fast,
she never heard
a little girl
laugh so loud.

Mr. Roger Mudd

I thought
Mama just might
be in love
with Mr. Roger Mudd,
I had never seen
her stare
at any man
the way
she stared at him.

Every night
after supper,
Mama would turn on
our old black-and-white
TV set
to watch the evening news,
and she would stare at
Mr. Roger Mudd
like he was

the most beautiful man
in the world.

I didn't think so.

"Listen to this man,"
Mama would say.
"He has news
of where Daddy is.
He has news
of Vietnam."

My brother and I laughed
at the idea of having
"mud"
for a name,
but we learned to be still
and to listen
to that man
and to look at the pictures
behind him
as he spoke.

Sometimes,
my brother would jump up
and stand close
to the TV screen,
hoping to catch
a glimpse
of someone
who just might be
our father.
"Hey, Dad,"
my brother would whisper
sometimes,
"where are you?"

Demonstration

They were in the park
all the time,
but we had never
really paid
much attention
before.

They were in the park
all the time
when we went out
for our walks
to the post office,
to the playground,
or just around the neighborhood
after supper.

Mama said they were
students, mostly,
students and
other young people.

They always seemed
happy,
wearing colorful clothes
and singing songs,
carrying signs,
clapping,
and dancing.

"Lucky kids,"
Mama said.
"I wonder
if they
even know anybody
in Vietnam."

Mama had a picture
in a gold frame
on a table
next to her bed.
It was a picture
of Daddy
in black-and-white,
wearing his Army uniform
and hat,
not quite smiling
but trying.

My brother used to
snatch up
that picture
and kiss it until
Daddy's face
was covered with smudges,
and Mama needed
to wipe the glass
clean.

I would
look at the picture
almost every day,
sometimes reaching out
with one finger,
touching Daddy's face
lightly,
never leaving
a single smudge.

Backseat Conversation

Mama was listening
carefully
to the news
on the radio
as she drove,
and raindrops were
drumming
loudly
on the roof
of our car.

"Do you think
Daddy knows
it's raining here?"
I asked.
"No,"
my brother said.
"Do you think

he knows
we're riding
in the car
right now?" I asked.
"No," my brother said.
"Do you think
he knows
Mama made
spaghetti
for supper
tonight?" I asked.
"No!" my brother said.

My brother
stuck his fingers
in his ears
and started
to hum.

"Do you think
Daddy knows
I'm forgetting
the sound of
his voice?" I asked.

Mama was listening
carefully
to the news
on the radio
as she drove,
and raindrops were
drumming
loudly
on the roof
of our car,
and my brother was humming.

Mama Tells a Lie

The old man
who worked at
the second window
in the post office
knew which kinds
of lollipops
we liked best.

Whenever he saw us
standing in his line,
he'd reach into
a big box
to pick out
three special flavors,
reds and purples, usually.

One day,
the old man held
two greens
and one purple

in his hand,
and I stared
at that purple pop,
licking my lips,
hoping
it was meant
for me.

Then I saw
Mama
lean closer
to the window
as the old man
held the purple pop
out to her.
Then I heard
Mama say
in a voice
too quiet,
"We haven't been getting
any mail."

And I knew
that my mother
was not telling
the truth.
I knew
for a fact
that we were getting
lots of mail,
bills and magazines
for sure.

I knew
we were getting
lots of mail.

Every Friday Night

Every Friday night,
just after
the television news
and just before prayers
and bedtime stories,
Mama
used to jam
the back of a kitchen chair
under the knob
of our front door
because
one of the men
who lived upstairs
would come home
drunk and confused
every Friday night
and think
our door
was his.

Prayers

Every night,
the three of us—
        Mama, my brother,
        and me—
would climb into
my brother's bed
to read a story
and say a prayer.

Every night
I closed my eyes
and listened to
the words,
the sounds,
and the comfort:
Our Father
Hail Mary
Angel of God.

My brother knew
all about prayer
and how to test
its power:
"Dear God,
help Mickey Mantle
hit a home run
whenever he wants to
even though people say
he's too old,
and help everyone
to come home
safely
from Vietnam,
and I mean
everyone.
Amen."

It was fine
if I was silent
after such powerful words;

it was fine
if I was too quiet,
too shy
to pray out loud.

Later,
lying in my own bed
with a night-light glowing
and my brother snoring,
I found my own way
of praying:
      our father,
            hail Mary,
                  angel of God,
    help me
    help me
    help me remember
    him.

The Wedding

Mama smiled a lot
at Daddy's sister's wedding;
everyone had
such a good time.

I danced
on the toes
and in the arms
of uncles and cousins
I never
knew I had,
and I'm pretty sure
I smiled a lot, too.

But no one
smiled
as much as
Mama,
who shook her head

and kept on
smiling
every time an uncle
or cousin
or friend
asked her to dance.

Christmas 1968

"This is
the best Christmas
ever!"
I announced,
sitting
right there
on the floor,
right there
in front of
our glowing,
shimmering
Christmas tree,
right there
in the middle of
heaps of torn wrapping paper
and red and green ribbons,
books and stuffed animals,
paint boxes and games,
skateboards and
hula-hoops,
everywhere.

Then I looked
at Mama
and my brother
and their
tightlipped
faces
and wondered
what in the world
was wrong
with me.

Suddenly,
it seemed,
the men
on the TV news
were angry—
not Mr. Roger Mudd,
who remained calm
and comfortable—
but other men
with important jobs
who screamed
at each other
about things
I did not understand,
like *escalation*
and *casualties,*
body counts
and soldiers who
could not
be found.

And there was Mama
staring
at the TV screen,
staring and
saying something
I did not want
to understand
at all:
"They have
no idea
where he is."

Telephone Conversation

My brother
held a finger up
to his lips.

Mama
was in her room
with the door
not quite closed,
and we stood there
in the hallway,
listening,
guilty.

Mama's voice
was steady
and strong
repeating
Daddy's name
and rank

and numbers
so many times,
steady and strong.

My brother and I
could do nothing
but run away
and try to disappear
when she finally
hung up the phone
and cried.

Different

I watched
the kids at recess
play their games,
the usual ones
like chase
and rundown
and dodge ball.

I leaned against
the side
of the school building
and shook my head
when kids asked
why
I wasn't playing.
"Don't feel like it,"
I said.

Later, I sat
at my desk
and put my head down
even though
no one
told me to.
I listened
to all the other
second-graders
get excited
about choosing jobs
for the next week.
I shrugged my shoulders
when it was my turn
to choose.
"Don't care,"
I said.

My father
was missing in Vietnam,
and I had heard
my mother
cry
for the first time
in my life,
and I
didn't know
what
to do.

Be Still

"Be still,"
Mama said,
which seemed like
an odd thing
for her to say
as we walked
through the park.

We stopped
and stood
silently,
the three of us—
> Mama, my brother,
> and me—
as we watched
and listened
to the students
and other people—

more than usual
and some
not quite so young—
chanting and shouting
loud and angry,
not singing
not dancing
not happy,
but scared,
like us.

Mama, Dancing

And then, at last,
the mail came
and Mama
    twirled
        and laughed
           and skipped
               and leaped
before settling down
breathless
to read out loud
the one letter
I remember better
than any
of the others,
with the end coming
at the beginning:
    How I love you,
        miss you,
           need you. . . .

I've been lost
in the jungle
for a while,
lost in the
fighting
and left behind,
but now I'm found
and coming home.
Did you dance a lot at the wedding?

Dreams

My brother
could not wait
for the day
to come.
He dreamed
the same dream
every night
for weeks
and woke up
every morning
with the same story
to tell:

"We're all lined up
at the Army base,
waiting for the plane
to land,
and then the plane comes
and the soldiers
get out,

and then
I see Dad,
and I break out
of line
and run
to him
faster than anyone
and I jump
right into his arms,
and it all seemed
so real
it just has
to come true."

* * *

Perhaps
I had heard
my brother's story
so many times
that I began
to dream

the very same dream
about my brother
breaking out of line,
running faster than anyone,
everything the same,
except in my dream
I run
even faster,
passing my brother
and winning the race,
jumping into
Daddy's arms
first.

Car Ride

"Sleep,"
Mama said.
My brother and I
fidgeted and squirmed
in the backseat
of our car.
"It will make
the trip seem
shorter."

We were
on our way
to the Army base
for the second time,
and I thought
it sounded like
a good idea
to dream my dream
one last time
before it all came
true.

But every time
I closed
my eyes
everything
was all mixed up.

Sometimes Daddy
looked like
his picture,
the one
next to Mama's bed,
his face frozen
in an almost-smile.
Sometimes Daddy
looked like
Mr. Roger Mudd,
his face
always moving,
saying the word
Vietnam
over and over.

And sometimes Daddy
looked like
someone I didn't even know,
his face blank,
as if he didn't know
me, either.

The Race

We stood in a line
at the Army base airport
in a section
roped off
like a movie theater
before the Saturday matinee.
We stood in a line
watching the airplane land,
and then watching
the soldiers
in green uniforms
shield their eyes
from the sun
and slowly
make their way
down the airplane stairs.

Then I saw him,
and I was under the ropes
running,

and I heard voices
behind me
telling me to wait,
shouting at me to stop,
but I ran, fast,
faster than anyone,
and I saw him
reach out to me,
and I heard him
call out my name,
and then I stopped,
still,
standing in one place,
because I saw him
and I heard him
and I knew that
I remembered him,
his face,
his voice,
and I knew
that Daddy remembered
me, too.

So, I stopped,
still,
standing in one place,
because I knew
I had already won
the race against
forever.

Almost Forever

Daddy comes to me.

He kneels
and places his hands
gently
on my shoulders,
studying my face.

> *Oh, Baby,*
> *I've been gone*
> *forever.*

His voice is
dry and hoarse
and sad.

Mama
and my brother
catch up to me,
gathering Daddy and me
in their arms.

"Almost forever,"
I whisper to Daddy.
"And then
you came home."

 *Becoming Joe DiMaggio*

**An American Library Association
Notable Children's Book**

**An International Reading Association
Children's Choice**

**A New York Public Library
100 Titles for Reading and Sharing Selection**

★ "Powerfully moving as it braids together
baseball, family, and the Italian American
experience." —*Booklist* (starred review)

★ "A powerful, glowing, unforgettable
achievement."
—*Kirkus Reviews* (starred review)

Hardcover ISBN 978-0-7636-1537-6
Paperback ISBN 978-0-7636-2444-6

Available wherever books are sold